This is a work of fiction. Any references to historical events, real people, or real places are used fictitiously. Other names, characters, places, and events are products of the author's imagination, and any resemblance to actual events or places or persons, living or dead, is entirely coincidental.

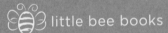 little bee books

251 Park Avenue South, New York, NY 10010
Copyright © 2019 by Little Bee Books
Manufactured in China TPL 0819
First Edition
10 9 8 7 6 5 4 3 2 1
ISBN: 978-1-4998-1012-7
littlebeebooks.com

Mighty Meg

4 BOOKS IN 1!

#1
MIGHTY MEG AND THE MAGICAL RING

#2
MIGHTY MEG AND THE MELTING MENACE

#3
MIGHTY MEG AND THE ACCIDENTAL NEMESIS

#4
MIGHTY MEG AND THE SUPER DISGUISE

BY Sammy Griffin

illustrated BY Micah Player

little bee books

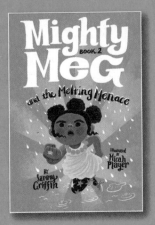

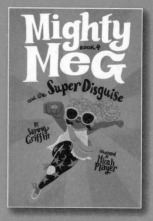

Mighty

BOOK 1

Meg

and the Magical Ring

BY
**Sammy
Griffin**

illustrated
BY
**Micah
Player**

Contents

Chapter One:
Meg's Perfectly Perfect Birthday Party

Meg's birthday was the most exciting thing to happen to her since her family went to Disneyland last summer. Turning eight was a big deal—like parades and fireworks big.

Her favorite people were there: Mom, her little brother Curtis, and her best friends Tara and Ruby. The only ones missing were Aunt Nikki and Uncle Derrick, but they would call Meg later.

Orange balloons hung from the lights in the living room. Orange-and-red streamers looped down from the ceiling above a stack of presents on the coffee table. A three-layer cake waited in the kitchen; Meg had already peeked at the peach frosting covered in purple sprinkles. She didn't have to check the freezer to know there was rainbow sherbet inside. Her party was practically perfect.

Curtis bounced on the couch, looking more excited than Meg. But that's just how her brother acted *all* the time—like his pants were on fire.

"How much longer?" he whined.

Tara and Ruby laughed while Mom came up behind him and put her calming hands on his shoulders, settling him into the cushions. "Be patient, C. It'll just be a few more minutes."

Like Curtis, Meg couldn't understand what was taking so long. Mom kept checking her watch like they were waiting on a pizza delivery or something. But they had already eaten dinner, cleared the table, and washed the dishes.

Being eight meant that Meg was more mature than Curtis and wouldn't pester Mom over and over again about when they would open presents, no matter how much she wanted to. Still, Meg watched the clock as she pulled Tara and Ruby onto the oversized recliner with her. The girls erupted in laughter as they became a tangle of arms and legs squished together.

When the doorbell rang, Mom pretended to look shocked and said a little too loudly, "I wonder who *that* is!"

Goosebumps spread on Meg's arms, and she sprang from the chair to follow Mom to the front door. Meg could tell something was going on, and she wanted to be right there when it happened.

Mom opened the door with a flair, and even though Meg had become a mature eight-year-old that day, she squealed in delight.

"Aunt Nikki!" she yelled as she barreled into her aunt's arms.

Meg's party had just become perfectly perfect!

Chapter Two:
Aunt Nikki's Adventure

Meg hadn't expected Aunt Nikki to come to her party because she had been on a scientific dig in Sweden. Her aunt was an archeologist, and she went on all sorts of adventures for her job. Meg wanted to be just like her when she grew up.

Meg wrapped her arms around her aunt's waist and squeezed tight. "You weren't supposed to be home until next week!" It had been two months since they'd last seen each other. Aunt Nikki's dreadlocks swooshed above Meg's head, and Meg breathed in her aunt's woodsy scent.

Uncle Derrick walked in and hugged Mom and Curtis while Aunt Nikki pulled Meg into the middle of the couch. Ruby and Tara settled down next to them.

"We found something amazing this time," Aunt Nikki said, "and we rushed home to study all the artifacts. Lucky for me, it also meant I could attend my favorite niece's birthday party."

Even though she had been waiting for the party to start, now that Aunt Nikki was here, Meg wanted to savor what was sure to be an incredible story. "Really? What did you find?" she asked.

Mom and Curtis sat across from them on the floor, a smile making Curtis's baby cheeks look even chubbier. Uncle Derrick stood behind them with his arms folded across his chest, impressed as always with his brilliant wife. Tara and Ruby leaned in closer to listen.

Aunt Nikki's voice deepened. "Our research took us to a little island off the coast of Sweden. There, we uncovered an ancient Viking burial ground where some believe their greatest warriors were put to rest."

Meg looked at her friends, sure that their astonished faces mirrored her own. She stared back at her aunt, whose gray eyes glowed. "On a hill above all the other graves sat a decorative tomb that clearly belonged to an important person. In it were the bones of what appeared to be a female Viking warrior."

"Whoa," Tara said. She looked from Meg to Aunt Nikki. "A *girl* warrior?"

"Yep," Aunt Nikki answered. "The very best kind."

Meg imagined what the warrior must have looked like with her armor and shield. She had almost forgotten where she was—in the middle of her own birthday party—when Mom interrupted her thoughts. "That's wonderful, Nikki, but I think it's time we celebrated this girl right here."

"Of course." Aunt Nikki stood and pulled Meg up next to her. She offered Ruby and Tara each a hand and pulled them up, too. "That's ancient history! Let's get back to the present where someone we all love is turning eight."

Chapter Three:
A Surprise Present

Everyone sat at the dining room table eating cake and ice cream. Curtis's face was so close to his bowl that a dot of peach frosting sat on his nose. Mom, Aunt Nikki, and Uncle Derrick all shared stories and laughed, catching up on the last two months while Meg and her friends took their empty bowls to the kitchen.

Noticing the girls had finished eating, Mom said, "What a fun party! But it's getting late and we should wrap things up."

"Or unwrap them!" Aunt Nikki said with a smile. "We can't forget the presents!"

They all moved to the living room and gathered around the coffee table, which was loaded with birthday presents. Meg knelt and opened Mom's package first, a bright new pair of orange sneakers with purple laces! She couldn't wait to zoom around the playground in them tomorrow.

Curtis gave her two new buttons to put on her backpack, one with a mustache and another with a llama that said "No Prob-llama." Meg had nearly covered half of her backpack already with her button collection.

Meg's dad sent her a beautiful shawl from Nigeria, where he was currently living. She couldn't wait to thank him during their next phone call!

Meg admired the illustrations in the book Ruby had given her. It was the latest in a mystery series by Meg's favorite author. Mom tried to hurry things along and told her she could thumb through the book later when she had more time.

Meg opened Tara's present, which was four bottles of bright nail polish. Her friend lined them up on the table, talking nonstop about their next sleepover and how they could paint and decorate one another's nails.

Meg picked her favorite color from the group. "I'm going to paint mine Bubblegum."

Ruby grabbed the bottle of sparkly green polish. "I'm painting mine Mermaid!"

"My favorite is Dragon," Tara said as she held out the shiny gold fingernail polish in her palm, oohing and aahing as if she were the star of a commercial.

Curtis snatched the last bottle of purple polish and held it high above his head. "Can I paint mine, too, Mama?"

The girls giggled, and Mom answered, "Maybe tomorrow, baby. Ruby and Tara's parents will be here soon to pick them up."

27

"But Meg hasn't opened our present yet."
Aunt Nikki reached into her pocket and set a
small box on the table in front of Meg.

Meg didn't even know that Aunt Nikki would be at her party. A present was an extra surprise. She studied the silver box, wanting to make this moment last as long as possible.

Tara clapped her hands. "Hurry up and open it."

Everyone watched anxiously.

"All right, all right," Meg said, slowly lifting the lid from the box. Inside, resting on a puffy bed of cotton, sat a thick silver ring with a scarlet stone. "It's . . . beautiful!" Meg whispered, hoping it would fit.

"We got it from a small market on the island," Aunt Nikki said.

Meg admired the fancy etchings on the silver band and slid it onto her middle finger, where it rested snuggly. A jolt shot from her finger to her arm and through her body, like an electric shock.

"Whoa," Meg said, feeling like something unusual had just happened.

Chapter Four:
Suddenly Sick

Aunt Nikki and Uncle Derrick stood up to leave. Meg went to give her aunt one last squeeze before they left, but she became dizzy and lost her balance. Ruby caught her by the arm and laughed. "I think someone had too much sugar."

Meg steadied herself and thanked everyone for coming. Mom's brow furrowed with worry. "Why don't you get ready for bed, sweetie? I'll make sure that everyone gets home okay."

Meg waved goodbye and weaved back to her room with Curtis on her heels. "Are you okay, Meg? You look a little woozy."

Her head throbbed, and her face felt flushed. "Can you please get me some water, C.? I'm thirsty."

While her brother ran to the kitchen, Meg changed into her pajamas and curled up in her bed. Curtis tumbled onto the covers next to her with a pink water bottle he had filled himself; she could hear the ice clinking inside.

"Are you going to be okay?" he asked, petting her long, spiral curls. Meg was feeling too sick to wrap her hair like she usually did.

"I'll be fine, Bubba." She called him by his baby nickname, and he let her because she felt sick.

Mom's swift footsteps sounded in the room, and soon her hand was pressed against Meg's forehead. "Hey, you have a fever," she said. "That came on pretty quickly."

With her eyes closed, it felt like Meg's bed had floated into the middle of the room where it spun around and around and around. Mom had her swallow some medicine and put a cool washrag on her forehead while Meg fought to keep her heavy eyelids from sinking.

Finally, Mom pulled Curtis from her bed, kissed Meg's forehead, and turned off the bedroom light.

Chapter Five:
Meg the Dream Warrior

Meg tossed and turned for a while before she finally settled down to sleep.

In her dream, she was on a lush island, standing at the edge of a cliff. A thick fog rolled in behind her as the sunset glowed pink on the horizon.

Meg's silver chain mail pulled at her shoulders and the nose guard on her helmet was distracting. But when she heard the galloping of horses behind her, she knew what she had to do.

Yelling out a war cry, she turned and ran directly toward the sound. Just as she saw the horses break through the fog, she leapt over the team, shooting to the sky like a powerful dragon.

She noticed every detail as she passed
overhead, as if she were flying in slow motion.
Whoa, Meg thought as she watched her legs
scissor in the air. The soldiers on horseback
looked up in amazement, a few reaching for
their bows and arrows to try and ground her.
Their leader cried out, and they struggled to
turn the horses around.

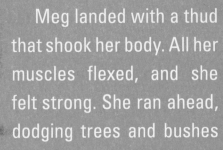

Meg landed with a thud that shook her body. All her muscles flexed, and she felt strong. She ran ahead, dodging trees and bushes with animal-like reflexes. It was only then that she realized she carried a long sword in one hand and a shield in the other. She used them to block branches and brambles. The scenery zipped past her in a blur.

Horse hooves pounded behind her, but she pulled ahead and the sound faded. The woodland rose into a mountain, and Meg leapt up onto it, scaling it like a panther. When the ground finally became too steep for the horses, she heard their leader command the soldiers to retreat.

She slowed to a jog and marched to the mountain peak. Her breathing was even.

When she reached the top, she could see the entire island dropping beneath her like a ginormous ball gown. Meg marveled at how far she had come in just minutes, without even breaking a sweat. A grin stretched across her face and she couldn't help but throw her head back and laugh triumphantly.

She saw the twinkling of distant stars in the dusky sky, and her new ring flashed in the dying sunlight.

Chapter Six:
Super at School

When Meg woke up the next morning, she was sad to discover she had only been dreaming. Her heart still raced from the excitement of her imaginary adventure, and she sighed as she wondered how it would feel to be a *real* Viking warrior.

Meg held her hand among the rays of sunlight pouring through the window and smiled to see that her ring was still real. Aunt Nikki coming home in time for her birthday hadn't been part of her dream.

It took some convincing, but Mom finally relented and let Meg go to school after her sudden sickness the night before.

"But I feel fine now," Meg told Mom, talking through a mouthful of waffle. "And I want to show off my new sneakers." She held out her foot to demonstrate.

"Okay," Mom said. "But go to the nurse immediately if you start to feel sick again."

Meg and Curtis took off for school down the sidewalk, waving at Mom, who pulled out of the driveway in her car and drove in the opposite direction toward her office. Max, an old golden retriever that belonged to their neighbor, Dixie Wickerson, followed them to the stop sign, like he did every day.

Curtis buzzed the whole way about his favorite dinosaur, the *Allosaurus*. "Did you know that its name means 'different lizard,' because it looks like a lizard and it's so much bigger than the other dinosaurs? It's like, Godzilla big."

Meg nodded, feeling like they were walking bug-slow. She wanted to break into a run like she remembered from her dream the night before, but she knew she shouldn't get ahead of her little brother.

Before they separated at school, she reminded Curtis that Mom would pick him up from Homework Club, his two-day-a-week, after-school program. Meg liked Tuesdays and Thursdays because it gave her a break from having to walk her brother home from school so she could spend some time with Tara and Ruby.

Curtis called out to a couple friends and followed them toward his first-grade classroom. Meg turned down the third-grade hallway and into Ms. Clements's class.

The room hummed with chatter as she walked back to her seat. When she pulled the chair out from her desk, it slammed into the desk behind her. The room grew silent and everyone turned to stare at Meg. She shrank into the chair and waited quietly for the bell to ring.

After class started and everyone's attention was on Ms. Clements, Meg turned back to look at the desk behind her; there were two baseball-size dents where her chair had slammed into the metal.

Did I do that? she wondered.

Chapter Seven:
The Disappearing Act

By gym class, Meg had forgotten about what happened that morning. Mr. Leonard announced that the class would be doing timed laps outside, and she was excited to run as fast as she could. He divided everyone into groups of five and had them take turns lining up on a chalk line he drew on the wide walking path that circled the playground.

The cool air nipped at Meg's fingertips, but she knew she would warm up as soon as she began to run. She stretched next to Tara, who was one of the fastest kids in class. "You're going to beat everyone with those cool shoes," her friend said, nodding at Meg's new, bright orange sneakers. They felt snug on her feet, and springy.

When Mr. Leonard called her group up, Meg stood on the outside of the track. Jackson, a tall boy from her class, stood next to her, crouching behind the line like an Olympic athlete waiting for the starting gun to go off.

"Good luck," Jackson said sarcastically to Meg and Tara. "You'll need it." Meg's stomach dropped, and she wondered when Jackson had grown so competitive.

Mr. Leonard counted down to the start of their run. When he shouted "go," Meg shot away from the line ahead of everyone else in her group. As in her dream, Meg didn't feel tired as she passed the climbing wall and swing sets. She wasn't even running as fast as she could. But when Meg realized she would cross the line before anyone else in her group was even halfway around the track, she knew something was different.

She slowed down and jogged to the finish line, still beating everyone else, but only by about ten feet.

"Wow! You moved like lightning!" Tara said, her mouth open in amazement. "How did you do that?"

Meg pretended to be out of breath so she wouldn't have to answer. But Tara's question still echoed in her mind. *How* did *I do that?* She snuck a peek at her ring, the scarlet stone blinking in the sunlight. It must have something to do with the Viking warrior ring.

Her super speed during gym was all Meg could think about for the rest of the day. She was so distracted by it that she didn't talk much to Ruby and Tara during lunch, and she gave them a silly excuse about having to go home right after school.

As she loaded up her backpack at her cubby outside Ms. Clements's class, Jackson called her name down the hallway. "It's Meg, the speed demon!" he yelled in a sneering voice. Meg's stomach twisted as Jackson neared, and she counted to ten, trying to calm her breathing as she waited for him to say something.

But when Jackson reached her, he looked all around, apparently unable to see Meg standing right there. His eyebrows bunched up, and then he shrugged and walked away. Meg turned to watch him go, and when she went to swing her backpack over her shoulder, she realized she couldn't see her own hands. Looking down at her body, Meg realized she couldn't see herself at all.

Meg had turned invisible!

Chapter Eight:
A Superpower Test

Meg went the back way home, cutting across the playground and through the big field that stretched across the empty blocks by her house. *What is happening?* she wondered as her mind spun from the craziness of the day. She ducked into a thicket of trees where she could be hidden while she tried to figure out what was going on.

In the grove, Meg could see birds perched in trees all the way across the field.

She closed her eyes and concentrated even harder. An argument between two brothers over a TV remote echoed in her ears. Meg's eyes snapped open to see where those boys might be, but she was too far away from any of the houses in her neighborhood to be able to hear something like that.

Meg told herself she needed to perform a few tests. She set her backpack down by the edge of the creek and jogged in place to warm up. Remembering her dream from the night before, when she leapt over the soldiers on horseback, Meg took a running jump over the creek.

She sprang high up in the air, easily clearing the treetops and flying toward the clouds. Her legs scissored beneath her and the air whooshed between her fingers as she started coming back down to the ground. Meg whooped when she landed and did a few more springy jumps toward the sky.

Remembering the two dents she had left in the desk at school earlier, Meg jumped into the middle of the creek and, pushing her shoulder against a boulder in the rushing water, she rolled it up one side of the creek until both she and the giant stone rested in the dry dirt. Laughing at the energy zinging through her body, Meg sped around the field as fast as she could, her body disappearing into a blur.

When she finally started to get tired, Meg took off her ring and dropped it into the outside pocket of her backpack. She had to know if it was the ring giving her these powers. Taking a running start, Meg leapt as high as she could, lifting only two feet from the ground before crashing into the dirt.

Her knee hurt, and her eyes stung from the pain. She grabbed a fallen leaf and used it to brush all the mud and gravel away from the scrape.

Meg pulled Aunt Nikki's present from the pocket of her backpack and slipped it over her finger again. She ran through all the things that had happened that day, holding up fingers as she counted:

Invisibility.

Super-senses.

Super-strength.

Super-speed.

A sharp tingle traveled down her back as Meg realized that her birthday ring had given her... superpowers!

Chapter Nine:
Choosing to Be Brave

Walking home through the field, Meg thought about what she should do with her newfound powers. She was too young to fight crime, and she was pretty sure Mom wouldn't approve of it anyway. Plus, Meg was a little shy sometimes, and she liked to keep to herself. Becoming a superhero might result in receiving a little more attention than she was comfortable with.

Meg kicked her way through the high grass as she realized that until she knew what she was going to do with these powers, she should keep everything secret. She shouldn't tell Mom and Curtis, or Tara and Ruby.

As she continued to think about her amazing discovery, a bubbling sound began to pound at her ears. *Someone must be boiling water for macaroni and cheese*, Meg thought. Super-hearing might get distracting after a while.

She went back to thinking about her powers. If a friend had a beautiful voice, wouldn't Meg encourage her to sing? Especially if her friend's singing could help other people be happier? Maybe part of having superpowers meant that Meg would have to use them to help people. She wasn't sure she was brave enough to do that.

The bubbling sound became so loud, Meg stopped walking to look around.

The small stream she had been following had gotten wider. She looked behind her to see that the gushing was coming from the middle of the creek, where the water gurgled like a geyser. It came from the same spot the boulder had been before she moved it.

The creek was now flooding over its banks, soaking Meg's new sneakers in the process.

This could be bad, she thought and backed away from the water. The stream suddenly became a narrow river with rough waves pulling bushes and sticks into its current. Backing up some more, Meg worried about her neighborhood. Would her house be swept away in a flood?

A dog's whimper turned Meg's attention forward. She saw that the water had pulled in old Max, her neighbor's dog, and he was being carried downstream. She had to help him! But her heart hammered in her chest, and her stomach twisted. She looked at her hands to discover that her fear had turned her invisible. Maybe Meg wasn't cut out to be a superhero after all.

83

Max's barking stopped and his head dipped beneath the water. *Max needed help now!*

Meg dropped her backpack from her shoulders and jumped to the bank closest to where Max had been pulled under. *Can I super-swim, too?* she wondered.

A few feet ahead, the base of a small tree dipped beneath the water line. Meg ran over to the tree and pushed against it until the trunk snapped, causing it to fall. Now the broken tree crossed the raging water like a bridge, and Meg carefully walked to where Max was struggling.

She scooped him from the water and leapt from her makeshift bridge. The force of her jump broke the tree in half, and its pieces were carried away. She laid Max on dry ground until he caught his breath and slowly stood. While he recovered, Meg jumped back to where she had moved the boulder earlier and rolled it back to the middle of the creek, plugging the geyser.

The gurgling sound of the water stopped, and within seconds, the river shrank back to its normal size.

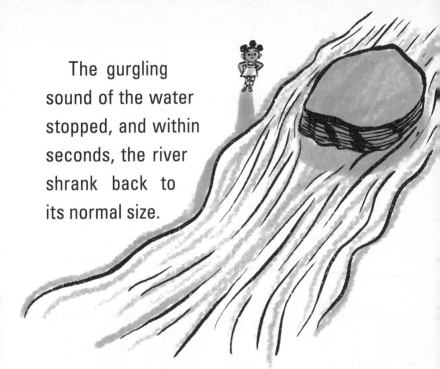

As Meg tried to dry Max off with a jacket she pulled from her backpack, Max licked her cheeks in thanks.

87

Chapter Ten:
Home in Time for Dinner

Meg and Max walked home slowly as the dog recovered from his scare. She led him across the street to Dixie's house and made sure to shut him inside the gate. She was done saving dogs for the night.

Crossing the street and heading toward her house, she thought the branches of their maple tree were glowing in the dusk. She shook her head, certain she was seeing things, but then the leaves flew away. Meg realized they weren't leaves at all, but hundreds of glowing moths.

Her superpowers weren't the only strange thing that had happened that day.

Meg thought back to the gurgling creek overflowing in the field. And now the tree full of glowing moths. What was happening in her ordinary town of Plainview?

Meg opened the door to her house and kicked her soggy sneakers off in the entryway. Curtis sat at the dining room table doing his homework, and she could hear Mom bustling in the kitchen.

"Is that you, Meg?" she called.

"Yes," Meg answered back, breathing in the scent of her favorite dinner—spaghetti with meatballs.

"It's starting to get dark out there!" Mom said, walking from the kitchen. She wiped her hands on a towel draped over one shoulder. She looked frustrated. "Next time, please tell me when you're staying late at Ruby's house so I can give you a ride home."

A knot formed in Meg's chest as she realized that keeping her secret from Mom meant she'd have to lie sometimes. "I'm sorry," Meg said, and the apology was more for her dishonesty than it was for being late.

"Are you hungry?" she asked.

"I'm starving!" Meg said, and *that* was the truth.

"Help your brother finish his homework first," Mom said. "And then we'll eat."

Meg peeked over Curtis's shoulder as he worked on a vocabulary worksheet. He only had one more sentence to fill in before he was done. "Although she was small, she was strong and _ _ _ _ _ _."

"There's only one word left." Meg tried giving him a clue instead of telling him the answer. She read the word's definition to herself: *possessing great and impressive power and strength.*

"Uh . . . mighty?" Curtis asked.

"Mighty!" Meg confirmed.

She realized that even though she was scared at first, she had still saved Max from drowning earlier, which was exactly the kind of thing a superhero would do. Maybe Meg could be brave enough to help people who needed it. Smiling to herself, Meg imagined wearing a fancy costume with a cape and double Ms on her chest, because she already knew what her superhero name would be. Mighty Meg.

Mighty

BOOK 2

Meg

and the Melting Menace

illustrated BY
Micah Player

BY
Sammy Griffin

Contents

Chapter One:
In the Hot Seat at Dinner

Meg snuck in through the side door of her house. She hung her jacket on a hook and kicked her shoes off in the mudroom.

"Meg?" Mom called from the kitchen.

She had hoped to make it to her room before anyone realized she was home. "Hi, Mom!" Meg walked over to where her mom stood by the stove, flipping grilled cheeses.

"How was school today, honey?" Mom looked tired. Her feet were bare, but she still wore her grey business jacket and skirt.

Meg leaned in for a half hug as Mom used the spatula in her free hand to flip grilled cheese sandwiches. "Good."

"What have you and the girls been up to?" Mom asked. "You haven't said much about Ruby and Tara lately."

The past week, Meg had been testing her new superpowers after school. She practiced in the open field by her house, using her super-speed to run around the field, her  super-strength to lift heavy rocks, and her heightened senses to see and hear faraway animals. She was even working on controlling her invisibility, so she would stop  turning invisible whenever she was scared. Meg hadn't been to either of her friends' houses to do homework with them like usual, but Mom didn't know that.

Meg shrugged. "Um . . . not much."

"Why don't you and Curtis set the table, and we'll talk more about your day over dinner."

Meg groaned to herself. She would have to figure out a way to get her brother to do all the talking. *Dinosaurs!*

She smiled. If she asked Curtis about *Velociraptors*, he would talk all night.

"Curtis!" Meg called her brother away from the TV in the living room. He reluctantly stood and came into the kitchen to help, the sound from his nature program still blaring in the background.

DAWN
OF THE
CHICKEN
O
SAURUS?

As Meg handed him the plates, he asked, "Did you know some scientists want to create a *Chickenosaurus*?" Curtis spent the next ten minutes talking about how cool a chicken-dinosaur would be. By the time he had turned off the television and sat down to eat, he was dinosaured out.

Mom ladled soup into their bowls and passed around the plate of grilled cheese sandwiches. Before anyone had even taken a bite, Curtis turned all the attention back to Meg as he said, "On my way to Homework Club today, I saw Tara and Ruby leave school without Meg." He slurped up a spoonful of soup, leaving a thick red mustache on his lip.

"Manners." Mom pushed Curtis's napkin toward him before turning to Meg. "Where were you, sweetie?"

Meg's cheeks flushed as she thought back to an afternoon spent jumping up into the tallest branches of the oak tree in the field by their house. It may sound like an easy feat for someone with superpowers, but apparently her super-jumping abilities did not come with super-coordination.

Meg had been practicing jumping all week, but it still took her quite a few tries to stick the landings.

"Looking for a book at the library," Meg lied, staring at her soup as if it was the most interesting thing she'd ever seen.

"Oh, really?" Mom swallowed a spoonful of soup before asking, "What book?"

"I didn't actually find it." Meg pulled at the crust on her sandwich. "It's a new book in a series, and the school doesn't have it yet."

"Ah, that's too bad," Mom said, and then she asked Curtis what he was reading in school these days.

Meg relaxed back into her seat, happy to have all the attention diverted away from her. But then she realized how easily Mom had believed her lie, and she felt even worse.

Chapter Two:
Hiding from Mom

After they cleaned up dinner and Mom signed her homework folder, Meg got ready for bed. She was in the bathroom brushing her teeth when Mom passed by on her way to Curtis's room. "I can't wait to hear about this new book when I tuck you into bed!"

Meg stood with her foamy mouth hanging open, toothbrush still in hand. What was she going to talk about? She glanced at her magical ring before she spat and rinsed, and then stared at her reflection again. If Mom found out about the ring and her superpowers, she would take it all away. Even if Meg wanted to use them to help people in trouble, Mom would still think it was too dangerous.

She could hear Mom's muffled voice down the hall reading a bedtime story to Curtis. Meg tiptoed out of the bathroom and into her own room. The bright yellow paint and ruffly bedspread always relaxed her. This was Meg's safe and happy place, no matter what happened outside her bedroom door. She lay down on her bed and stretched out, tracing the plastic stars on the ceiling with her eyes.

"Good night, C." Meg heard Mom begin her nightly tucking-in ritual with Curtis. She imagined her turning on his night-light and blowing him a kiss before heading down the hall to Meg's room. Mom would bombard her with questions that Meg could only answer with lies.

The knot in her stomach returned and Meg looked down to find she had completely vanished! She still couldn't choose when she turned invisible. In fact, she had almost no control over when it happened at all! Mom walked through the doorway, and Meg watched her step into her room and check all the corners for her.

"Meg?" Mom put her hands on her hips and cocked her head to the side, her eyebrows bunched together in confusion. "Where did you get to now?"

Mom swept about the room, her robe catching air and looking like a cape blowing out from behind her. "Meg? Where are you, sweetie?" Mom's footsteps padded through the house and Meg climbed under her covers and concentrated on becoming visible again.

During her superpower practices earlier that week, she had discovered that when she turned invisible, if she imagined being visible in her mind, it made it easier for her to become visible in real life. Her fingers wiggled before her eyes, and Meg released a long sigh.

"Meghan Asha Hughes!" Mom sounded frustrated now. "Where are you?!"

Meg turned toward the wall and closed her eyes. She could avoid all Mom's questions if she pretended to be asleep when she was found in her bed.

Meg could hear Mom's footsteps as she walked down the hall and entered her room.

Mom whispered, "Well, I'll be darned." She silently moved through her tucking-in ritual with Meg, bringing the covers up over her shoulders and kissing her on the cheek before whispering, "Sleep tight, my strong and wise warrior."

Meg couldn't help but smile as Mom walked out of her room. It was as if Mom's nighttime blessing had come true.

Chapter Three:
A Field of Icicles

Curtis was antsy that morning, bouncing in his seat as he shoveled cereal into his mouth.

"Slow down, C." Mom watched him from the kitchen as she stood by the toaster, waiting for her bread to pop.

Meg pulled the crust from her honey toast and crumbled it over her scrambled eggs while Curtis scrunched his face at her plate. "That's gross," he said, his mouth full of mushy Sweet Flakes.

"*That* is disgusting," Meg responded, rolling her eyes and pointing at his bad table manners. Maybe he would be more respectable when he turned eight.

"I want to get to school early today," Curtis said. "There's a tetherball championship, and I'm going to win it."

"Oh, are you now?" Mom sat at the table with her coffee and toast. "Then you two better hustle!"

Curtis dashed from the dining room, and Meg knew that was her cue to hurry up and finish breakfast. She didn't want her brother nagging her to leave.

By the time Mom had cleaned up Curtis's breakfast, they were all ready to walk out the door. Curtis rushed ahead. Meg grabbed her sack lunch and her backpack as she ran to catch up, careful not to use her super-speed where someone could see her. They both blew Mom kisses as they passed the driveway and jogged down the sidewalk.

Once they were out of sight, Meg used her super-speed to catch up with her brother. In a flash, she was right behind him. He never even saw her coming.

"Whoa, when did you catch up?" he asked.

Before she could answer, Curtis stopped. They had reached the spot where Meg had been hiding out after school that week, practicing her superpowers. But instead of an open field, the tall grass was covered in icy spikes! They looked like stalagmites, those rock formations that rose from the bottom of caves like spears. These jagged pieces of ice were nearly as tall as Curtis.

"What are those?" Curtis asked.

"I don't know." Meg thought back to the geyser that had flooded the stream, and the glowing moths she'd seen last week. "This makes no sense. It's too warm for ice."

Small puddles were already forming around the snowy cones as they melted in the new-day sunlight. Meg guessed that they would be gone by lunchtime.

"Hey! You're going to miss the tournament."
She nudged Curtis, who blinked hard before
snapping out of his trance.

"That's right!" Curtis squared his backpack
and took off running for school.

With her super-speed, it didn't take much
for her to keep up with him, and as she ran,
Meg's concern about the strangle icicles
continued to needle at the back of her mind.

Chapter Four: Melting Danger

Meg and Curtis traveled down the shortcut that led to the playground behind their school. It was a narrow dirt path lined with trees. Normally, the sun shone through the leaves and it was a pretty walk. But today the path was really foggy. Curtis had to look down at his feet to make sure he didn't trip. He could barely see in front of his face.

As they passed through an opening in the fence, the fog lifted and Curtis saw a crowd gathered around the tetherball courts. He took off running. Meg watched him go, standing on the spot where the dirt path turned to pavement.

Something about the fog just wasn't right. Meg used her super-sight to peer through it. Usually the barrier next to the path was steep and layered with stones, but with her powers, Meg could see that the stones were being held up by a thick ice shelf! It was as if a troll or goblin had created the perfect booby trap, stacking the stones behind a melting wall. And just like the field of snowy spikes, the ice was slowly thawing. A trickle of water was already flowing onto the path in front of her.

Meg studied the ice shelf, just as puzzled by it as she had been by the icy stalagmites earlier. Why would there be strange ice formations in two different places this close to spring? Regardless of what had caused the ice to appear, once the ice melted, the stones would topple onto the path. Anyone traveling on the shortcut to or from school could get hurt!

No one would even be able to see the danger through the fog. Meg thought about telling a teacher, so they could just shut down the path. But how could she explain that she could see the ice shelf without revealing that she had super-sight? If only she could break the ice, causing the rocks to fall harmlessly while no one was around. Meg bent her legs, ready to leap into action, but kids began walking down the path. The shortcut would be crowded with students until school started.

She would have to solve this problem another time.

Chapter Five: Super Secrets

$\mathcal{M}$eg waited on a bench outside the front of the school until Tara's dad pulled into the drop-off lane and let her friends out. For as long as Meg could remember, she and Ruby had been like sisters separated by three blocks. And when Tara moved onto Ruby's street in the second grade, they all began hanging out together and had been best friends ever since.

Sometimes Tara's and Ruby's parents drove them to school while Meg walked with Curtis. After waving goodbye to Tara's dad, Tara and Ruby skipped down the walkway with their arms locked together. Meg felt jealous, knowing they'd been spending time without her after school all week. Even though she knew it was her choice and not theirs, she still felt sad.

"Meg!" The girls called out to her and ran to the bench.

Meg forced a smile and gave them both a big hug.

"We've missed you." Ruby looped her arm through Meg's so she could join their chain.

"Yeah!" Tara agreed. "We were starting to worry that turning eight had made you too cool for us."

"I've just been busy after school lately,"
Meg said. "That's all."

"We're just kidding, Meg." Ruby bumped
shoulders with her so she'd know they were
playing. "But we're dying to know what you've
been up to!"

"Definitely!" Tara leaned over to meet Meg's eyes. "It has to be more exciting than homework and no-bake cookies." Being reminded of their after-school routine made Meg feel a little homesick, even though she hadn't really gone anywhere.

"Not really," Meg said, even though what she had been doing instead of hanging out with her friends had been pretty exciting. Keeping this super secret from her friends made her feel even worse, and Meg started looking forward to the first bell.

The girls walked into the school together, their footsteps echoing in the foyer.

"You can tell us all about it at lunch," Ruby said.

Tara nearly cut Ruby off when she added, "We're going to blast you with questions so we don't miss anything!" Both her fists splayed when she said blast, like she was making explosions with her hands.

Meg laughed nervously as they turned down the third-grade hallway. All of these questions were making her anxious. First her mom, now her friends—it was hard keeping secrets. Concentrating on being visible, Meg wondered how she could avoid answering their questions while still working on a solution for the melting ice. Spending lunch in the library might help solve both problems.

Chapter Six:
Hiding out in the Library

If she stood on her tiptoes and looked out the back window of the library, with her super-sight, Meg could just barely see the ice shelf. It had already melted halfway, and a few stones had fallen onto the path. At this rate, the ice would break away just as kids were walking home!

"Meg, sweetie," Mrs. Johansen called to her from the checkout desk. The library was empty, and they were the only two people in the room. "You don't want to eat lunch with your class?"

Kids could eat lunch in the library if Mrs. Johansen was there. The librarian was one of the nicest people Meg knew, and she had bright blue eyes and long white hair. She sometimes wore her glasses like a necklace, attached to a string of colorful beads.

It was Mrs. Johansen's idea to open the library during lunch, so all kids felt like they had a quiet and safe place to eat and spend recess if they wanted. Meg nodded in response to Mrs. Johansen's question and held up her lunch bag as if it were proof.

Meg sat down and pulled her peanut butter and honey sandwich from the bag. She needed to figure out how to destroy the ice shelf and the threat of a stone avalanche before lunch was over.

Meg scribbled down ideas as she ate, crowding a small slip of paper with mostly silly solutions. Her plan had to be perfect: She needed to get onto the playground, fix the ice shelf while no one was on the path, and then come back, all unnoticed. She tapped the pencil to her temple as she thought.

151

"Got it!" she whispered. She jumped up and went to the nonfiction section of the library, searching for just the right book. When she found the one she wanted, she took it over to the checkout desk.

"A book on ice? In the springtime? That's an interesting choice," Mrs. Johansen said, stamping the inside before handing the book back to Meg.

The first bell rang as Meg returned to her table in the back. She threw away her trash before quietly opening the back window and leaving her library book on the window ledge. Meg took a deep breath. *This had better work*, she thought.

Chapter Seven:
Questions in Science Class

Meg nearly collided with Tara and Ruby as she darted from the library into the science classroom after lunch.

"Hey, where were you?" Ruby asked, her mouth pouty.

"Yeah." Tara looked annoyed. Of the three girls, she had the shortest fuse, although she was also the quickest to stand up for her friends. "We looked all over for you."

"Sorry," Meg said, and she meant it. She didn't want to upset Tara and Ruby. "I had to do some research at the library."

Luckily, there wasn't much time to talk before the bell rang and science class started. Tara and Ruby both turned away from Meg to face the front of the class, but their frustration hung in the air like an invisible cloud.

Mr. Fester paced the front of the classroom as he continued their discussion from yesterday about strange natural phenomena, like fire tornadoes, underwater crop circles, and sailing desert stones that left long trails behind them in the sand. Of all the science teachers Meg had ever known, Mr. Fester looked the most like a science teacher from a TV show: He wore glasses with thick, dark frames, had curly red hair, and wore collared shirts with pockets full of writing utensils.

This couldn't be more perfect, Meg thought. Her hand shot up into the air.

"Meg?"

"What about a field of icicles. Could that be a thing?"

Meg could hear a handful of students behind her snickering at her question.

"Actually." Mr. Fester stopped and nodded his head thoughtfully. "It *is* a thing. Only they're not called icicles, but *penitentes.*"

"Penny-what?" someone called from the back of the room.

"Pen-i-ten-teys." Mr. Fester sounded the word out slowly. "*Penitente* is the Spanish word for penitent, which means someone who is sorry for something. People thought these icy formations looked like a group of people praying for forgiveness."

He rushed to the tablet on his desk, which was connected to the whiteboard, and searched for pictures. He showed images of the same thing Meg and Curtis had seen that morning: fields of jagged ice cones pointed at the sun.

"They occur in high altitudes when dew forms, but temperatures are below freezing." Mr. Fester had stopped on one picture where the white *penitente* stood out against a bright blue sky. He gestured at the picture enthusiastically. "The sun turns sections of the snow into vapor without melting, leaving behind the formations you see. Some of these snow spikes can be as tall as thirteen feet."

The ones Meg and Curtis saw had not even been half that tall, although they may have started out taller and melted down. Also, Plainview was in a valley, not a high altitude place at all. Not to mention, it was not very cold. It was nearly spring! *Penitentes* in Plainview sounded practically impossible.

Jackson, seated behind Meg, groaned as Mr. Fester went on. "*Penitentes* are found mostly in South America—this is a picture from the Andes Mountains. Can you see how they look a bit like people praying?"

"Brainiac." Jackson leaned forward to whisper into Meg's ear. "You better *pray* he's almost done answering your boring question."

Meg sank into her seat as Mr. Fester droned on.

Chapter Eight: Hall Pass

After showing a video on the northern lights, Mr. Fester assigned a short worksheet for students to complete by the end of class. Meg knew this was her best chance to sneak out to stop the ice shelf from causing an avalanche!

She asked Mr. Fester if she could go to the bathroom, and he gave her a hall pass. Meg snuck back into the library where Mrs. Johansen stood at her desk giving the second graders a lesson on genres, the different types of stories you could read.

The librarian was so fascinated with her topic that Meg was able to slip into the back of the group and blend in with the class. When Mrs. Johansen turned her back to grab sample books to show the students, Meg tiptoed backward until she could duck between a row of books and eventually crawl to the window she'd left open during lunch.

Waiting until just the right moment, when Mrs. Johansen and the second  graders were completely distracted, Meg climbed onto the windowsill and popped the screen out from the window. Placing her legs through first, Meg sat on the ledge. With a little grace, she dropped from the second-floor opening and landed on her feet with a thud. She didn't have much time to lose.

Meg sprinted toward the ice shelf. It had nearly dripped away to release the stones, which now tottered on a thin sheet of ice. With her super-sight, she could see a man through the fog. He was speed-walking  at the far end of the path. Meg had to act fast. She had already been gone from class for too long. How was she going to clear the path?

169

On the other side of the rocks, away from the path, she spotted a canal. If she could make the rocks fall that way, the danger would be gone. Searching for something to help her, she found a wooden post lining the shortcut.

Like a professional weight lifter, Meg pulled the wooden post from the earth and hoisted it above her head. Holding it high, and ignoring the worms and bugs that dropped down from it, she jumped over the stones to the top of the ice shelf. She nearly lost her balance on its slippery surface.

Meg found herself wishing again that super-coordination was a part of her superhero package.

Carefully, she turned around and faced the stones being held back by the ice. Using the post like a plow, Meg bulldozed the stones down off the shelf and into the canal on the other side. When she turned back around to admire her work, she saw that only a few small rocks were now dotting the path. The shortcut was safe again!

The man coming down the path would be able to see her soon. Luckily, he was concentrating on the ground as he drew closer. Before he looked up, Meg sped away.

Meg darted back through the playground at super-speed, right up to the library window she had slipped through minutes earlier.

Chapter Nine:
Super Sneaky

𝕸eg climbed up the wall so she could peek into the library through the open window. Mrs. Johansen stood at the desk, checking out the second graders' books.

While Mrs. Johansen was busy, Meg shimmied through the window.

After she snuck inside, Meg put the window screen back on, pulled the hall pass from her back pocket, grabbed the library book from the ledge, and walked toward the library doors.

As she passed the front desk, Mrs. Johansen's head snapped her way and the librarian called out, "Meg? When did you come in here?"

This had all been part of Meg's plan. In response to Mrs. Johansen, Meg held her hall pass up in one hand and the library book in the other. "I forgot my book," she said.

The librarian nodded and called after Meg on her way out the door, "See you later!"

As Meg turned the corner heading back to science class, she practically collided with Mr. Fester. He let out a whoop of surprise before he said, "I was just coming to find you. You've been gone for a while, Meg. Are you feeling okay?"

"Yep." She smiled, and then showed him the library book, called *Strange Frozen Phenomena*. "Sorry. I was really curious about the ice formations we talked about in class." And for once, she wasn't lying! Meg still wanted to know how ice had formed in Plainview at the start of spring.

"I'll let it go this time," Mr. Fester said with a relaxed sigh. Meg could tell he was pleased at her interest in his lecture that afternoon. "But next time, you need permission to go to the library."

"Thank you, Mr. Fester," she said, and led the way back to class.

Meg was relieved that she had solved the melting ice problem, but she still had one more super task she had to complete by the end of the day.

Chapter Ten:
Caught Speeding Home

When the final bell rang after her last class, Meg rushed to her cubby in the hallway. Lately, she had been grabbing her backpack and speeding away from the school before her friends had a chance to see her leave. But today was different. Instead of running away from Tara and Ruby, she was trying to find them.

She waited by Ruby's cubby outside Mr. Fester's class, where the girls used to meet before Meg had gotten her superpowers. Ruby's name sparkled above her cubby, cut out from purple construction paper and dusted with gold glitter.

Soon, Tara and Ruby walked from their classroom into the hallway, laughing with their heads ducked together. Meg felt worried as she watched them, but then she reminded herself that *she* had left her friends; they hadn't left her.

When the girls saw Meg, they both stopped and stared.

Tara folded her arms across her chest, still looking annoyed that Meg had avoided them at lunch. "Oh, you're here. What's wrong?" she asked.

"Nothing," Meg said, picking at the strap on her backpack before looking at her friends. "I was just hoping I could hang out with you guys after school today."

Tara relaxed, and her arms dropped down to her sides. Ruby squealed and pulled Meg into a crushing hug. "Of course you can! It hasn't been the same without you!"

Tara joined in, and the three friends jumped up and down in their little huddle.

After the girls spent the afternoon making no-bake cookies and working on their homework at Tara's house, Meg started her four-block walk home. The big smile that had been on her face since school let out made her cheeks ache.

Meg tightened the straps on her backpack and looked around to see if anyone was watching. The sun had dipped below the tree line, and the cool air bit at her fingers and nose. She zipped her jacket up all the way and waited for a car to pass before she took off down the road, running so fast, the air whizzed in her ears.

Mom and Curtis pulled into the driveway just as Meg was jogging up the steps to the house. She stopped and waited for them to catch up.

As Mom stepped closer, Meg noticed that Mom looked at her differently, almost like Meg was an exhibit at the zoo. "Since when did you become an Olympic runner?" she asked suspiciously.

Meg looked down at her orange sneakers and her cheeks prickled with heat. "I've always liked to run." While that was true, Meg couldn't help but wonder how much her mother had seen.

"I stopped by Tara's house to pick you up a few minutes ago, but she said you'd left." Mom unlocked the door and waved Meg and Curtis inside ahead of her. "They were surprised you weren't still on their block since you'd just barely started walking home."

Meg shrugged and kept walking past Mom. "I'm going to put my backpack away," she said, turning to look at Mom before heading up to her room. The suspicious look from before had been replaced with a smile.

"Hurry back for dinner," Mom said as Meg skipped off with her backpack.

After she ducked into the safety of her bedroom, she dropped her backpack on the floor. Meg would have to be much more careful from now on.

She admired the scarlet ring on her finger and smiled to herself. She had saved people from getting hurt on the shortcut today, and that left a happy, warm feeling in her chest. Meg spun in a circle before collapsing onto her bed.

Maybe she could handle this superhero thing after all.

Mighty

BOOK 3

Meg

and the Accidental Nemesis

BY
Sammy
Griffin

illustrated
BY
Micah
Player

Contents

Chapter One:
Early Morning Fright-ball

Meg and Curtis stood at their school's back fence, studying the playground with their feet planted. Meg's arms were crossed. The sun was rising in the sky, but the air was still cool enough to bite at their bare arms.

The bell would ring soon, but there was still time before school started, and they each needed to decide what they wanted to play.

Curtis eyed the four
square courts busy with
games and a short line
where kids waited their

turns to play. In the
middle of the field, third and
fourth graders played touch
football, while a small crowd
scampered around in a race
that seemed to end by touching
the top of the climbing wall.

"I'm going over there."
Curtis pointed at
the football kids
running toward
the bench they
were using as one
of their goalposts.

"No way." Meg swung an arm out to hold
him back. "Those are big kids playing football,
and you're just going to get hurt."

"I AM a big kid," Curtis said, but hung back anyway. "And you're not the boss of me!"

"You're six." Meg walked toward the playground, making sure her little brother kept pace with her. "And I am the boss of you when we're at school. Mom said so."

Curtis grumbled as they marched around the huddle at the edge of the field. Jackson stood in the middle, giving his teammates instructions. "We're gonna crush 'em!" he yelled, and the small group of kids around him cheered. They ran back toward the other team, lining up in the middle of the field.

Curtis took off toward the slide, and Meg went to the front of the obstacle course, hoping to join the next race. As she waited, Meg played with the magical ring sitting on her finger and wondered if she could win without using her super-speed.

She watched as the touch football game started again. Jackson took the snap. He ignored his teammates who were waving their arms for him to pass it to them. Instead, he cradled the ball and ran down the field. He dodged through the other team members, most of them looking confused, like they weren't really sure how to play football after all.

As he neared the bench goalpost, Tommy Hedrich from Meg's reading class stepped into Jackson's path, both arms raised to try and tag him. But instead of slowing down, Jackson sped up, like Tommy was a finish line tape he had to bust through. Even though the action was far away, Meg could tell that if neither boy backed down, someone was going to get hurt.

Meg ran over from her spot, kicking up bark as she zipped to the field using enough of her super-speed to get there quickly, but not enough to draw extra attention to herself. The other players slowed her down as she wove around them to avoid any collisions. Meg got there just in time to see Jackson ram Tommy with his shoulder.

The smaller boy crumpled to the ground in a heap, Jackson landing heavily on top of him. Tommy yelled out in pain, and the teacher on field duty blew her whistle and ran over to check on the two boys.

It took a few minutes, but Meg finally helped Tommy up. As soon as he stepped onto his left leg, he cried out in pain. Two of Tommy's friends slung his arms over their shoulders and walked him to the nurse's office while Jackson kicked at the grass, juggling the football from one hand to the other.

"Jackson!" the teacher snapped. "You know we only play touch football on school grounds. What you did was very dangerous. Please come with me to the principal's office."

Chapter Two: Football Banned

Meg slid her homework folder into the desk and admired her ring. The sun pouring through the window caught the scarlet gem and reflected a constellation of stars onto her desktop. She smiled and sat down to wait for the tardy bell.

Kids around her stood in the aisles between the desks, most of them chatting about the football play that hurt Tommy Hedrich's leg. Ms. Clements walked in, and the room quickly grew quiet. She turned her back to the class and began writing on the whiteboard.

Just as the bell rang, Jackson slunk into the classroom and pushed his way to his seat in the back. Yumi Sato, a girl with straight black hair and glasses, was bent over to grab a pencil she had dropped under her desk. Jackson bumped her and Yumi nearly fell to the ground. He mumbled, "Get out of my way, Four Eyes." Yumi got back up and sat in her seat, the pencil forgotten by her feet.

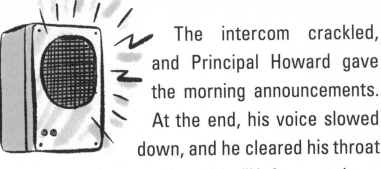

The intercom crackled, and Principal Howard gave the morning announcements. At the end, his voice slowed down, and he cleared his throat before he said, "Unfortunately, a student was injured playing touch football on the playground before school this morning. To make sure something like this doesn't happen again, students will no longer be allowed to play football at Plainview Elementary unless supervised in gym class."

A few of the kids in her class groaned, and Meg snuck a peek over her shoulder to see Jackson's reaction. His chin was resting on his hands, as if he was too tired to pay attention. But Meg knew better. The pushing and name-calling meant he was also upset about what had happened that morning. Whether he felt bad that he had hurt Tommy or he was just mad that Principal Howard had banned football, Meg couldn't tell.

Back in second grade, Jackson had been a quiet, small kid who listened to teachers and played nicely with everyone. Lately, he seemed to get upset easily, and lots of kids were afraid of him. Jackson acted like a kid practicing to become the school bully.

Meg looked at her ring again. This was just the kind of problem her superpowers might be able to help solve. She wasn't sure how yet, but she was going to find a way.

Chapter Three:
Jackson Dominates

At recess, Meg, Ruby, and Tara played mini Olympics on the monkey bars, competing to see who could do the best tricks. Meg loved the superhero practice and had gotten good at crossing the bars upside down, swinging from rung to rung on the backs of her knees.

"Are you taking gymnastics?" Ruby asked. "Because that looks really hard."

Tara tilted her head at Meg and squinted her eyes against the sun. "You're too good, Meg. This isn't fun anymore." She turned and started walking toward the field where the kids who used to play football were now playing kickball. "Let's go join the kickball game," Tara called to her friends over her shoulder.

Ruby followed, and Meg reached the last rung and swung down from the monkey bars in a cherry drop. Hiding her powers from her best friends was getting harder.

They reached the baseline where a group of girls waited for their turn at the plate while Jackson pitched the ball for the boys' team.

Tara leaned into Ruby and Meg and whispered, "Jackson's gotten so big this year. No wonder he hurt Tommy's leg when he ran into him."

The rumor was that Tommy's mom had called the school to let them know he had sprained his knee and wouldn't be back at school for a couple days.

"He tells everyone he's dominating his wrestling team, too," Ruby said. "And he runs all the time, like super-fast, through the neighborhood." Jackson lived on Ruby and Tara's block. The girls saw him walking to and from school, and sometimes just playing in the cul-de-sac.

"Come on, Slow Poke!" Jackson yelled at Marissa Sanders from atop the yellow frisbee that someone had set down as the pitcher's mound.

Tara wrinkled her brow at her friends and said, "I don't want to play kickball if Jackson's going to be mean to us."

"Me neither," Meg said. "Do you want to play four square?" There wasn't much chance she would reveal her superpowers there, unless she accidentally popped a ball with her super-strength.

They walked off the field as Jackson rolled the ball, and it barreled toward Marissa. Even though she kicked hard, the ball didn't
come off her foot that quickly, and it only rolled a few feet from the pitcher. Jackson

raced to grab it, his face twisting as he picked up the ball. He brought the ball over his head with both hands and hurled it at Marissa. It swooshed by her head, blowing her hair back on one side before hitting the bottom of the chain-link fence lining the field. The throw was so strong that the ball stuck under some loose fencing at the bottom.

A boy in the outfield yelled, "Hey! No head shots, Jackson!"

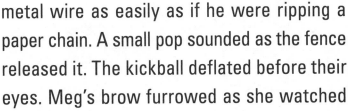

Jackson shrugged and jogged to the fence where he yanked the ball from the clinging metal wire as easily as if he were ripping a paper chain. A small pop sounded as the fence released it. The kickball deflated before their eyes. Meg's brow furrowed as she watched Jackson drop the floppy ball into a garbage can and run to the four square courts without saying anything to his team.

229

Chapter Four:
Attack on the Trees

eg's gym teacher was out sick, so the substitute teacher, Coach Cathy, shooed them all outside. Before they could play, they each had to pick up ten pieces of garbage on the playground.

Meg and Tara waved their trash bags into the wind and they caught the air like brilliant white kites. All around them, kids searched for garbage while they talked, laughter echoing across the field.

Tara ran ahead and called over her shoulder to Meg, "I bet there's trash by the back fence." Meg 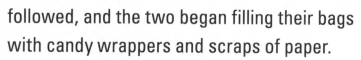 followed, and the two began filling their bags with candy wrappers and scraps of paper.

In the back corner of the field, Jackson and his best friend Porter dug through the underbrush in a small patch of trees, clearing the trash that had gotten stuck there. When they stood, Porter beat his chest like Tarzan and jumped onto a small sapling that bent under his weight. Jackson laughed and climbed onto a bigger tree next to it, getting a few feet off the ground before Coach Cathy blew her whistle and waved them down.

Tara rolled her eyes as Jackson jumped from the tree, landing on his feet and flexing his arms like a bodybuilder. "Show-off," she muttered loudly enough only for Meg to hear.

Meg watched as Porter and Jackson swatted at each other. Messing around with his friend, Jackson looked harmless. Meg couldn't help but wonder if what had happened with Tommy that morning and then while playing kickball after lunch had just been accidents.

Meg and Tara ran a few feet closer as a piece of newspaper blew across the grass. The girls raced to reach it, Meg holding back her super-speed so her friend wouldn't become suspicious. Tara beat her to the paper and stuffed it into the bag, raising her first in triumph. The girls giggled before catching sight of Jackson and Porter karate-chopping the little tree.

234

"Hey, stop that!" Tara called at them.

Jackson looked over his shoulder at Tara and smirked before he roundhouse-kicked the trunk. Meg saw his leg flex before it hit the wood, a surge of strength traveling from his foot to the tree. There was a snapping sound as the trunk cracked and broke in half. Jackson stood still, looking at the pale wood inside the bark of the broken tree, just as surprised about it as Tara and Meg were.

The girls walked closer to the patch where the boys stood, frowning at the broken sprig.

235

"Jackson and Porter." Coach Cathy
came up behind them and *tsk*ed. "That was
uncalled for! You're lucky this is a wild patch
of trees the school is planning to tear down."

Meg watched Jackson shrug for the
second time that day. "Sorry," he said. "I . . .
didn't mean to."

She remembered the shock she'd felt at
her own superpowers when she had first
gotten the ring. Could Jackson be struggling
to control a newfound strength? Meg cocked
her head as she looked from Jackson to the
broken tree, wondering if she had more in
common with Jackson than she ever thought.

Chapter Five:
King of the Mountain

Tara complained about the broken tree as they walked to Ruby's house after school. She thought Jackson should pay for a new one to take its place.

Meg interrupted, "But Coach Cathy said the school is going to take those trees down anyway."

"Still," Tara said. "That poor little tree didn't deserve that."

"Can we talk about something else?" Ruby asked. "Like the kindergarten teacher's pink hair, glitter slime, or, I've got an even better idea—our dance-off!"

Even though her friends were happy to change the subject to the dance-off they would hold that afternoon since no one had much homework, Meg couldn't stop thinking about Jackson. Why did he seem so grouchy lately? How had he suddenly gotten so strong? Was it possible he had superpowers of his own?

Jackson walked ahead of them with his friends, Porter and Dan, but Meg knew if she concentrated, she could hear what they were talking about. They were excited about a movie they wanted to see on Saturday. Porter asked Jackson, "Will you be at your dad's house this weekend?"

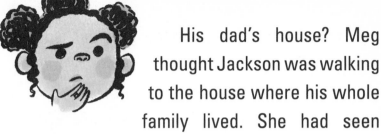

His dad's house? Meg thought Jackson was walking to the house where his whole family lived. She had seen them all there before. Meg wondered if they were moving.

Jackson grumbled, but didn't answer. Instead, he said, "Want to play king of the mountain?" He climbed atop a stone wall surrounding the corner house, and Porter and Dan scrambled up behind him.

"Okay, now try to push me off," Jackson said. "Whoever makes me jump down becomes the new king of the mountain." The wall looked as tall as Meg's shoulders, and the boys wobbled a bit as they tried to keep their balance. Jackson's friends were soon on either side of him, and they jokingly swatted at Jackson, not trying very hard.

The girls slowed down as they reached the boys' game, and when Jackson saw them, he held a karate pose and kicked Porter in the leg—hard. Porter groaned and stepped back, almost falling off the wall and into the yard on the other side.

Dan looked around Jackson to see if Porter was okay, and then said, "Hey, that's not cool, Jackson."

Jackson grabbed Dan's arm and twisted it around so that it bent at a funny angle. Meg remembered the accident she hadn't been able to stop that morning and decided she couldn't let anyone else get hurt. She leapt to the top of the wall behind Dan and leaned around him to wrench his arm free from Jackson's grip. Dan jumped down to where Porter waited, and the two friends took off without Jackson.

The king of the mountain studied her and said, "Whoa! Wanna play?"

"No way!" Meg jumped down. "If you're not nice," she called up to him, "no one's going to want to play with you anymore."

Ruby and Tara stared at Meg before the three of them hurried down the sidewalk to Ruby's house.

Tara said, "How did you do that, Meg? You jumped onto that wall like a goat or something."

"A goat?" Ruby asked. "Don't they climb, not jump?"

"That's not the point," Tara said, turning back to Meg. "It was like you flew to the top of the wall without even trying. And then you twisted Dan's arm away from Jackson like a professional wrestler."

"She didn't exactly fly." Ruby put her hand on Meg's arm. "But it was pretty impressive."

"Whatever," Tara said as they reached the steps to Ruby's house. "Meg, you totally need to share your monkey bar secrets, goatlike tricks, and bully-smackdown strategies with us."

Meg shrugged, a nervous smile pulling at the corner of her lips. Ruby changed the subject back to their dance-off, and Meg breathed a small sigh of relief.

Chapter Six: Super-Nemesis

The three girls danced as Ruby's playlist blared from the portable speakers in the living room. Tara and Ruby held hands and swung in a circle as Tara complained about how mean Jackson was acting lately. Ruby wondered if Porter and Dan would still be his friends after that brutal king of the mountain game on the way home from school.

Tara said, "If he's going to be that mean to his friends, can you imagine what he would do to his enemies?"

After his football crash, the popped kickball, and the rush of strength Meg thought she saw when he broke the tree, Meg shivered a bit at the thought of a bully having superpowers. *Is that how villains are made?* she wondered. *Could Jackson become a supervillain and my nemesis?*

The girls stopped talking to focus on their dance moves, and Meg moonwalked to the music, sliding backward until she slammed into a marble column Ruby's dad used to display his grandmother's vase. The column rocked, and Meg steadied the vase so it wouldn't fall and break.

When the moment passed, Meg looked up to see Ruby and Tara staring at her.

"How did you move that?" Ruby asked, pointing at the dark marble column next to Meg. "It's super-heavy. Dad can't even move it by himself."

Tara walked up to the column and moved the vase to the floor. She pressed against the column, testing its weight. Ruby stood next to her, and the two girls pushed against the marble with their combined strength, their faces twisted with the effort. Meg's own face flushed, and her cheeks stung.

"Seriously. How did you move this column?" Tara asked.

"I don't think I did," Meg said, quickly thinking for a reason the column would have rocked when she bumped it.

She joined her friends, and the three of them pushed against it together. Meg made sure to hold back her strength. "See?" she said. "I must have just accidentally hit the vase instead."

Tara and Ruby looked at each other, exchanging suspicious glances.

"I don't know, Meg," Tara said, her face expressionless. "I'm starting to think you're an alien or a cyborg with superhuman strength."

The three girls busted up laughing, Meg louder than her friends.

As Tara put the vase back on the column, Ruby suggested, "How about we make some no-bake cookies now?"

Meg followed her friends into the kitchen. She wasn't sure which to worry about more: Jackson's bullying behavior, or the growing struggle to hide her superpowers from her best friends.

Chapter Seven:
Playground Games

The next morning, Meg and Curtis stood at the back of the playground again. The weather was warmer, and the sun toasted their shoulders as they decided what to do with the time remaining before the morning bell rang.

Where kids had been playing football yesterday morning, a small soccer game moved back and forth across the field. Other kids swarmed the tetherball poles, and all the four square courts looked full.

There was a bigger group of kids running through the obstacle course across the playground. Without saying anything, Curtis took off toward the race.

"C.," Meg called after him. "Hey, wait up!"

Her brother looked over his shoulder, waved at Meg, and then bolted toward the group like he had just engaged his hyperdrive. Meg searched the crowd for her friends, but Tara's dad sometimes dropped them off right before the bell. It looked as if Meg would have to play alone this morning.

Arriving at the obstacle course just as the previous race was ending, Meg watched Jackson and Porter stand in the tower at the top of the slide while everyone gathered below for instructions. Apparently, Jackson's karate chop to Porter's leg had been forgiven. Meg huffed to think his friends were okay with him being so mean to them.

Jackson used a booming outdoor voice. "This is how it works. The race starts at the other side of the climbing wall. After you climb up and down both sides, you cross the monkey bars, and then go over the geodome, down the zip line, and up this slide." Kids buzzed with excitement, a couple first graders even clapped their hands. "Once you get up here, you have to get past me and Porter before crossing the rope bridge to reach the tower on the other side. First one who does, wins." He shrugged like it was the easiest game on the planet.

261

Meg cocked her head and frowned at Jackson. Just yesterday he had tried to hurt a bunch of kids. Did he really think anyone believed that pushing past him and Porter at the top of the slide would be easy? Or safe?

The entire group ran to the climbing wall to take their marks.

Curtis was one of them.

Chapter Eight:
A Mighty Mistake

Before Meg could object, Jackson yelled, "Ready, set, GO!"

Curtis leapt onto the climbing wall. Even though he didn't have superpowers like Meg, her little brother had always been athletic and strong. And he liked to win. Curtis jumped halfway down the back side of the climbing wall and sprinted to the monkey bars.

After everything that had happened yesterday, Meg was certain Jackson hadn't learned a thing from Tommy Hedrich's sprained knee and the football ban. He was going to keep playing rough.

Her brother led the race, dropping from the monkey bars and scampering to the geodome. Meg had to stop Curtis before he reached the top of the slide where Jackson and Porter waited, guarding the entry to the rope bridge. Her only option was to reach Jackson first, so no one would get hurt.

Meg ran to the climbing wall to join the race herself. She bound up the side, swinging from one grip to the next using just her hands. When she reached the top, she dropped to the other side without climbing down. In a flash, she was at the monkey bars, taking them three at a time. A group of second graders on the geodome complained that big kids shouldn't get to play as Meg zoomed ahead of them.

Curtis dropped from the zip line and ran for
the slide while Meg waited for the handle to
return to her. Super-speed flowed through her
legs as she swung them hard to propel herself
to the end, and in seconds, Meg completed
the zip line and reached the slide right behind
her brother.

Curtis was halfway up. To beat him to the top, she'd either have to show off her superpowers or be sneaky. Meg decided that in this crowded race, it was best to be sneaky.

She scampered beneath the slide where it would be harder to see her and climbed the underbelly, holding the sides as she scuttled to the top. Swinging up the side of the slide, she stuck the landing, face-to-face with Jackson and Porter. They had both been watching Curtis climb the slide and were startled when Meg suddenly appeared before them.

Porter took a step back, away from Meg, as Jackson grabbed Meg's wrists and tried pushing her back into the tower over the slide. Without thinking, Meg yanked her hands free, trying to get away from Jackson. Her super-strength made her skin tingle.

Her strength was too much for Jackson, and it knocked him down. He fell on his back, a puff of air leaving his mouth noiselessly. The wind was knocked out of him. Jackson struggled to take a breath while he looked at Meg, terrified. That's when Meg realized that Jackson didn't have superpowers after all. Meg came to a standstill. Had she just hurt someone with her powers?

Curtis reached the top of the slide just as Jackson caught his breath.

"Are you ok?" Meg asked Jackson as her little brother ran past, stomping across the rope bridge to the tower on the other side.

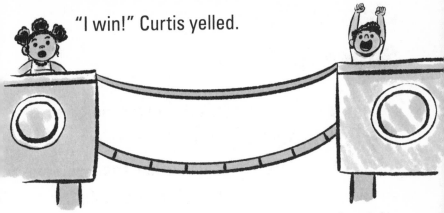

"I win!" Curtis yelled.

Jackson's pale face slowly regained its color, his eyes now wet with tears.

Chapter Nine:
Super-Sad

Meg slogged through the rest of the morning feeling like a brick was stuck in her stomach. As she held Tara's feet while her friend did sit-ups in gym class, Meg watched Jackson out of the corner of her eye, wondering if this was how he felt after accidentally spraining Tommy's knee the day before. She had never thought she would use her superpowers to hurt someone. Even though it had been an accident, Meg still felt horrible about it.

At lunch, she pulled at the crust from her peanut butter and jelly sandwich, and tore off tiny bird bites that she dropped into her mouth. Ruby and Tara chatted about the prizes for their genre challenge in reading class. Kids who read a book from each of the assigned genres were put in a drawing for different prizes.

Tara told Ruby, "If I win, I'm going to choose the candy basket."

"Hmm." Ruby popped a grape into her mouth, chewed, and swallowed before saying, "I would pick the movie pass."

Her friends giggled about the best and worst prizes while Meg looked around the lunchroom for Jackson. He sat alone in the back corner, saving spots on either side of him with an apple and a milk carton. His lips were turned down in a frown as if everything bad that had happened was hanging from the corners of his mouth.

Meg left the cafeteria and found Jackson's friends in the hallway outside the lunchroom, talking to Ms. Phoebe, the school counselor. Meg was so focused on Jackson's friends that a few minutes went by before she realized she had been using her super-hearing to listen in on their conversation.

"Just keep being good friends," Meg super-heard Ms. Phoebe say. "That's the best thing you can do for him."

Porter and Dan nodded, and Ms. Phoebe put a comforting hand on each of their shoulders. "Having your parents go through a divorce can be hard for a kid. I've talked to him about being gentler to those around him even though he's upset, and I think he's starting to understand. But it'll take some time for Jackson to act like himself again."

Meg remembered how angry Jackson was when Porter asked if he would be staying at his dad's house this weekend. Jackson wasn't pushing people around because he had superpowers or wanted to be mean, he was upset that his parents were getting divorced. Meg was four when her own parents got divorced. She didn't remember much from that time, but she knew that she would sometimes get sad and pretty upset.

She looked back at Jackson eating by himself. The brick in Meg's stomach turned from guilt to empathy, as Meg realized that Jackson's super-strength was really just super-sadness coming out as something other than tears.

Chapter Ten: Franken-enemy

The bell rang, and Meg rushed from Ms. Clements's class to her hook in the hallway, where she stuffed the homework folder from her cubby into her backpack. She looked up to find Tommy Hedrich standing outside Mr. Fester's class with his mom. Tommy stood stiffly with a dark brace on his knee while his mom took a small stack of books from Mr. Fester.

Meg watched silently from her hook, listening to them talk about Tommy's recovery and the makeup homework he would do while resting his knee at home. Jackson approached them hesitantly, and Meg began to walk down the hallway, slowing as she passed.

Tommy said, "It still hurts a little, but I'll be back at school next week."

Jackson looked at Tommy and said, "I'm sorry, Tommy. It was an accident. I didn't mean to knock you over and hurt your knee."

Tommy gave a little smile and said, "It's okay. Thanks for apologizing."

The chill that had settled in Meg's chest earlier warmed a bit. Jackson sounded sorry for hurting Tommy. Maybe Jackson wasn't really a bully after all.

Meg waved at Tara and Ruby standing outside their classroom up the hall. Today her friends would go to Ruby's without her. Curtis didn't have Homework Club after school, so Meg would walk her brother home where a teenager next door, Latisha Gold, would babysit them until Mom got home from work.

Feeling light and happy now that Jackson was looking less and less like a bully, Meg took off toward the first-grade classrooms to find Curtis. The hallway echoed with chatter and smelled like sweat. Her brother walked tall with his friends, still beaming about winning the race against the big kids that morning. "Hiya, Meg."

"Hi, guys," Meg said to his friends and then waved Curtis away from the group so they could head home. As she turned around to leave, she bumped right into Jackson, who had been standing right behind her. He glared at her.

"You know, that was some trick you pulled this morning." His mouth twisted around his words like they were sharp.

"It was an accident," Meg whispered, hoping to remind him of his own apology to Tommy minutes ago.

Jackson was one of the tallest kids in her class and towered over her. Even though she finally knew that Jackson didn't have superpowers, it didn't stop her from being a little afraid of him.

"You can't just go around hurting people like that." He talked like he had just appointed himself Bully Patrol. He leaned a little closer to her and added, "And I'll make sure it doesn't happen again."

Suddenly, all her words got stuck in her throat. Jackson was making her feel like she was dangerous, when she had been the one trying to protect people from him! She told him it was an accident. She was sorry, but he was the one being unsafe. It was all wrong now.

Meg felt something bubble up inside her. It was like the feeling she got when she was about to use her powers, but this time, she knew she wouldn't be running, jumping, or turning invisible. She looked Jackson right in his eyes.

"I'm sorry for knocking you down. That was an accident. But you had no right to grab me or push me. And if you try to do that to me or anyone else again, I'll be there to stop you!"

Before Jackson could even think of a response, Meg grabbed her brother's hand, stepped around Jackson, and walked away. Curtis looked at his sister in awe, and then gave her a high five.

When Meg and Curtis reached the shortcut they used to get home, Curtis skipped ahead. Even though she had stood up for herself, Jackson's warning made her uneasy. She had finally come to understand why he had been acting so mean, but he was still angry with her anyway. After all her work to keep Plainview and her school safe, Meg realized she may have accidentally created her own nemesis. Did Jackson really think Meg was a threat to anyone? Having superpowers was so much harder than she thought it would be.

Curtis disappeared ahead of her, the sun shining through the trees and casting moon-shaped shadows on the ground. As the birds sang and the wind hummed through the trees, Meg decided that, for now, she would try to be positive and remember Jackson's sincere apology to Tommy. Things could always change for the better. Besides, the counselor said it would take some time for Jackson to feel like himself again.

For now, Meg wanted to focus on what she could control. Even though Jackson didn't turn out to be a real supervillain, there were still other things out there that the people of Plainview needed Meg to protect them from.

She ran to catch up with her brother. *Well*, Meg said to herself, *no matter what comes next, I know I'll be ready for it.*

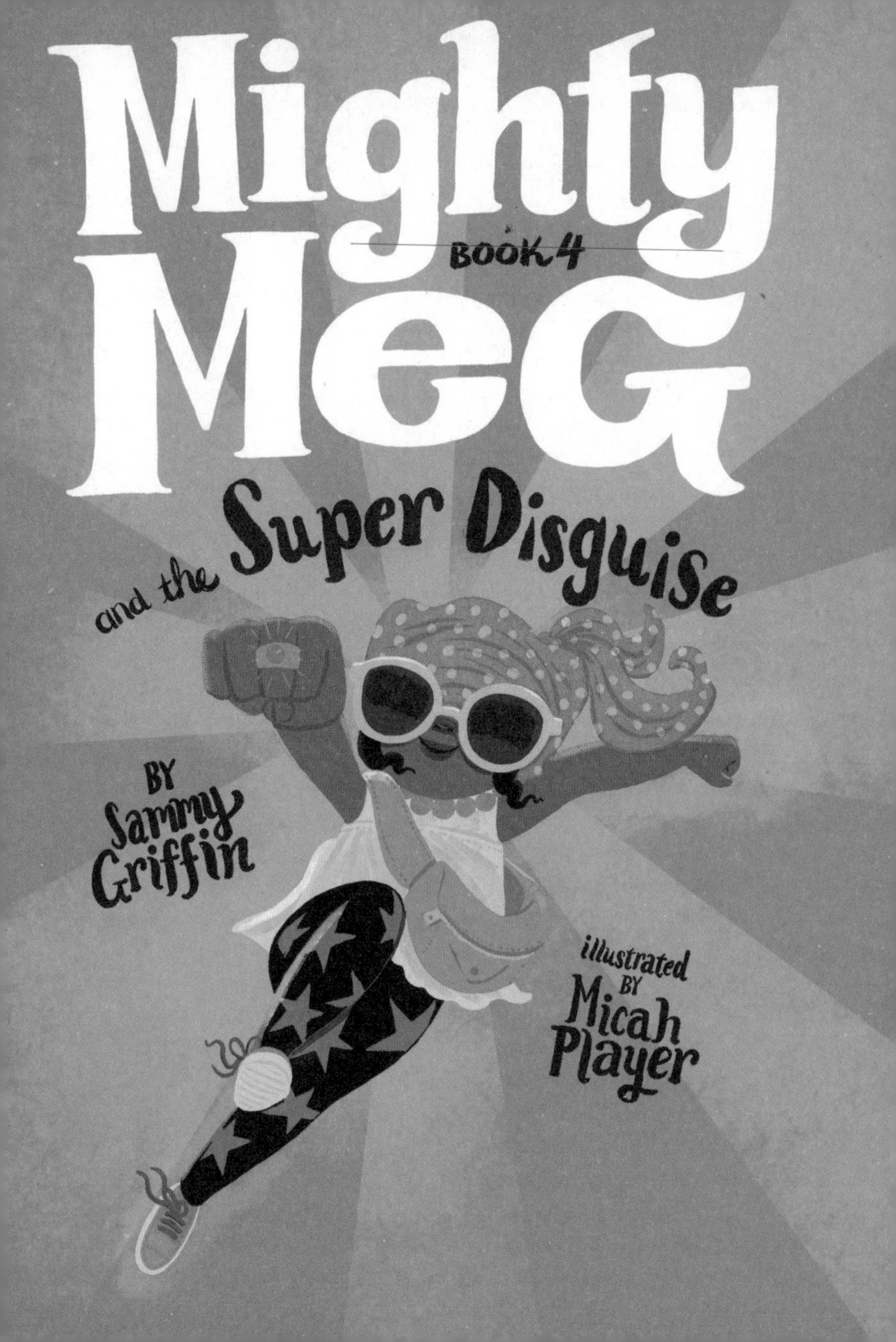

Mighty Meg

BOOK 4

MeG

and the Super Disguise

BY
Sammy
Griffin

illustrated
BY
Micah
Player

Contents

Chapter One:
Startling Sinkhole

The sun pricked at Meg's bare shoulders as she walked home from school with her little brother, Curtis. As they passed an empty field, the breeze picked up a voice crying and carried it to Meg's superpowered ears.

She looked at Curtis, who continued to skip over the sidewalk lines. The superpowers she got from her magic ring were hard at work again, and she needed to figure out what they were trying to tell her. Meg had to follow the sound.

She hurried, calling out to Curtis, who lagged behind. "Come on, C.! Let's check out the park."

Meg could now tell that the cry came from a mom calling to her child somewhere around the small playground two blocks outside Meg and Curtis's usual path to school. Turning down the street, Meg rushed Curtis along as they neared the park. A swing set and slide stood in a circle of dark playground bark. It was empty.

A tall mom with long hair frantically searched the parking lot of the apartment complex next door. "Caroline! Caroline!" she yelled. She ran between the parked cars, and dropped to her knees to search beneath them. Even without her super-hearing, Meg could tell that the mom's voice was starting to give.

"We should help her look," Curtis said.

Meg nodded just as another sound reached her. A whoosh echoed in her ears, followed by a gasp and a small cry. Her head snapped to where the noise came from, opposite the parking lot. A small, wooded area lined the back side of the playground.

"You help the mom look," Meg said. "I'm going to double-check the field."

"But it was empty," Curtis complained.

"I'll come right back," Meg promised, feeling her brother's eyes on her as she ran toward the slide. When Curtis's calls joined the mother's, Meg jetted toward the trees behind the park using her super-speed.

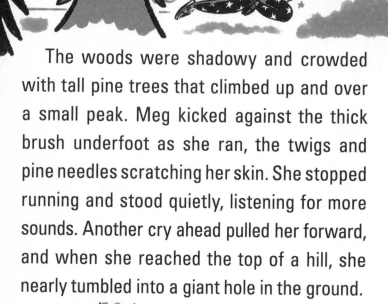

The woods were shadowy and crowded with tall pine trees that climbed up and over a small peak. Meg kicked against the thick brush underfoot as she ran, the twigs and pine needles scratching her skin. She stopped running and stood quietly, listening for more sounds. Another cry ahead pulled her forward, and when she reached the top of a hill, she nearly tumbled into a giant hole in the ground.

She peered inside,
but the hole was dark,
crowded with roots and
branches of broken trees.

311

"Help," a weak voice called from below. When Meg's eyes adjusted to the darkness, she saw a small girl cradled in between two tree trunks.

Chapter Two: Sly Rescue Mission

As Meg brainstormed ways to rescue the girl from the sinkhole, she could hear Curtis and Caroline's mother draw closer. She had to figure out how to get Caroline out of the hole fast.

If Meg dropped to Caroline's perch, her weight might push the trees farther down the hole. Plus, Meg had to somehow pull Caroline free without revealing her own identity. She knew that once people discovered what she could do, someone was sure to take away the magic ring that had granted her superpowers.

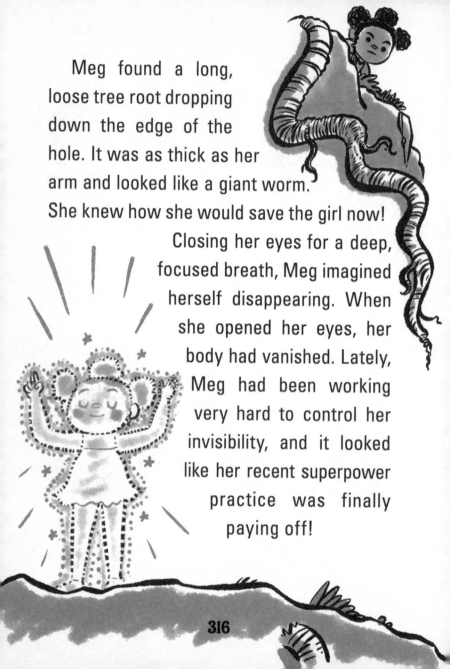

Meg found a long, loose tree root dropping down the edge of the hole. It was as thick as her arm and looked like a giant worm. She knew how she would save the girl now!

Closing her eyes for a deep, focused breath, Meg imagined herself disappearing. When she opened her eyes, her body had vanished. Lately, Meg had been working very hard to control her invisibility, and it looked like her recent superpower practice was finally paying off!

Meg took another deep breath, and when she exhaled, she backed away from the sturdy forest floor and jumped into the dark sinkhole.

Meg waved her arms in front of her, grabbing for the tree root and letting it slide through her hands until she was just above the girl. Her fingers clamped down on the rubbery wood, and she swung 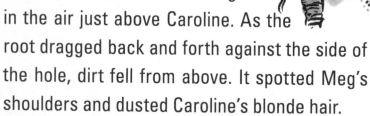 in the air just above Caroline. As the root dragged back and forth against the side of the hole, dirt fell from above. It spotted Meg's shoulders and dusted Caroline's blonde hair.

Meg stared at her dirty arms, the soil covering her clothes. She could see herself again! Try as she might to imagine herself invisible, all her superpowers seemed to be channeled into her super-strength. Caroline huddled below, ducking her head as the dirt continued to sprinkle down. Meg would have to figure out another way to make sure Caroline didn't see her.

Meg reached down, wrapping one arm around the little girl's waist while clutching the root with the other. Caroline yelped in surprise, but then she relaxed against Meg.

Somehow Meg needed to escape the sinkhole while holding Caroline. Meg dropped onto Caroline's perch, and with all her strength, she leapt up, launching them toward the hole's opening as the tree trunk collapsed into the pit beneath them.

Still holding Caroline from behind, Meg set her gently onto the ground. Before the girl had a chance to look around, Meg jumped as far from her and the sinkhole as possible, landing in a cluster of trees bordering the park. She listened closely as Curtis and Caroline's mother continued to call for the girl. They sounded like they were almost to the top of the hill.

Using her super-speed, Meg raced back toward Curtis and Caroline's mother, slowing down when she saw them crest the hill. Putting on her most convincing expression of surprise, Meg ran toward Curtis, meeting him at the sinkhole.

Caroline cried in her mother's arms, trying to explain that she had been in the hole one minute and then yanked from it the next. Caroline could've sworn someone saved her, but when she was outside the hole, she was all alone. Meg enjoyed the feeling of relief that spread across her body like goose bumps. The girl was safe, and so was her secret.

"Thank you so much for your help," Caroline's mom told Curtis, who smiled shyly.

But when her brother looked up at Meg, his eyes cut into a suspicious glare. "Why are you so dirty?" he asked her.

Meg looked down, causing dust to fall from her head. She brushed the dirt from her arms and answered. "I fell down the hill when I was trying to catch up to you."

Curtis chuckled. "You're such a klutz," he said.

Meg chucked him on the shoulder. "We should go home before Latisha starts to worry about us." Their babysitter would call Mom if they didn't make it home on time.

As they walked home, Curtis talked nonstop about the sinkhole. While he talked, Meg realized that even though she had managed to save Caroline without being caught, she still needed some kind of plan for using her superpowers in public. Meg needed a disguise.

Chapter Three:
Dancing and Daydreaming

During recess the next day, Meg, Ruby, and Tara practiced their new dance routine. The girls swung their hips to a song Ruby had made up, stopping on the eighth count to throw out their arms and jump as high as they could. Meg was careful not to jump too high. They strutted backward a few steps before spinning to face the opposite direction, taking turns doing high kicks.

A small group of second graders had gathered to watch them, oohing and aahing as the friends moved in sync. Jackson had stopped behind their admirers to glare at Meg before his friend Porter called him over to play tetherball. He lasered Meg with one last scowl and then jogged away.

"From the top," Tara cried out, and the three girls took their places again. Ruby yelled out a quick countdown and started to sing, the girls stepping through their routine almost as naturally as breathing.

As they danced, Meg thought about the close call with Caroline yesterday, and how Curtis and the girl's mother could have crested the hill just as Meg leapt from the sinkhole with Caroline in her arms. They both would have known that no ordinary girl could save someone from a gaping hole in the ground like that.

Using her superpowers in public put her at risk of being discovered. But Meg had to use her abilities to help people, and that meant that sometimes others would see her. She needed a costume or a disguise to prevent that from happening.

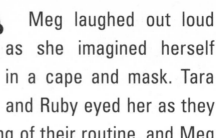

Meg laughed out loud as she imagined herself in a cape and mask. Tara and Ruby eyed her as they spun to the ending of their routine, and Meg covered her mouth to stifle more giggles.

After they relaxed their jazz hands, the small audience asked if the girls could teach them the routine, and Meg, Ruby, and Tara grinned at the idea.

The girls walked through their steps slowly this time, and while they did, Meg decided that a simple disguise would be much better than a full costume. She just needed to keep her real identity a secret, and a disguise would help her accomplish just that.

Their new students laughed as they matched the girls' movements, and Meg forgot all about her superpowers as she enjoyed a fun, ordinary recess.

Chapter Four:
The Case of the Multiplying Sinkholes

On the way to Ruby's house after school, the girls caught a glimpse of the park Caroline had wandered away from the day before. Two big city trucks had pulled onto the grass surrounding the playground.

"What's going on over there?" Ruby asked.

"That's where Curtis and I found the girl who fell into the sinkhole," Meg said. "It was ginormous, like a bottomless pit."

"Let's go check it out!" Tara yelled as she darted ahead of her friends without waiting for them to answer.

Meg and Ruby followed after her, their shoes slapping on the pavement. Like the day before, the playground was empty.

"Where's the sinkhole?" Tara whispered, even though there was no one else nearby to hear her.

Meg pointed past the trees. "Over there!"

The girls slowly made their way into the woods, Meg leading them toward the sound of people talking. As they neared the top of the hill, the girls crouched behind a thick pine so they wouldn't be shooed away by the adults.

The three workers were standing around the dark sinkhole. They peered over the edge cautiously, as if a mud monster might leap out at them.

The tallest of the three workers said, "We'll pour a layer of cement, fill the hole with sand, and then top it off with some dirt." They all nodded, agreeing with the plan.

As they backed away from the hole, a fierce groan echoed behind them. The girls watched in horror as a patch of trees was swallowed by the earth, dropping out of view and into the ground. The workers hollered in surprise and sprinted away from the spot, stopping just shy of the girls' hiding place.

"What was that?" one of the men asked.

"Another sinkhole," the woman responded. And then she added, in a whisper, "What is going *on* out here?"

Meg was thinking the same thing. She remembered the strange river that had formed out of nowhere, nearly drowning her neighbor's dog, Max. And then there were the ice formations that appeared by her school on a warm spring day. Now, Plainview had these scary sinkholes. It seemed that ever since Meg had gotten her magic ring, unusual things had begun happening around her town, and each one was more dangerous than the last.

Chapter Five:
More Secrets

The girls spent another recess dancing on the playground. After the bell, they walked back toward the school building, all of them out of breath. Ruby and Tara chatted excitedly about creating a new routine.

Ruby, pink-cheeked and smiling, said, "I know Curtis doesn't have Homework Club today, but why don't you come over after school so we can practice?"

Meg groaned. "Sorry, guys. Latisha's expecting us." Even though she knew her babysitter probably wouldn't mind the break, Meg had planned to work on her disguise after school and didn't want to put it off.

Tara stopped outside the school doors, jutted out a hip, and frowned. "Really? Even if your mom gives you permission?"

Tara pushed ahead of Ruby and Meg as the three girls stumbled into the hallway, which echoed with laughter and crowded conversations.

Meg said, "She wouldn't want to trouble Ruby's mom any extra."

"It's no trouble," Ruby insisted, pulling on Meg's arm. "Come on, Meggers! We could practice for the school talent show—it'd be so much fun!"

Meg hated avoiding her friends like this, especially when it required a little dishonesty, but until she could fully control her invisibility with her other superpowers, she needed a disguise. "Sorry, guys. Mom has a super-important meeting this afternoon, and I'm not allowed to interrupt unless it's a real emergency. But we can totally get started tomorrow." And there was the white lie—Mom hadn't told Meg about any important meetings today.

Tara grumbled under her breath and Ruby rolled her eyes as the girls walked into science class.

This wasn't the first time Meg had lied to her friends because of her magic ring. When she first discovered the superpowers it gave her, she had avoided them for a week in order to practice her new skills.

The girls sat at their desks, a triangle of seats with Tara in back and Meg and Ruby in front of her. They twisted in their chairs, out of habit, ready to chat until class started. But since they were disappointed that Meg wouldn't be coming over after school, the girls shrugged sadly and looked away.

Guilt pressed on Meg's chest, making her heart achy. She hated keeping secrets from her best friends. Would she have to hide her superpowers from them forever? The thought of keeping a never-ending secret made Meg tired and grouchy. She trusted Ruby and Tara more than almost anyone else in the world. Surely, she'd be able to share her secret with them someday.

Chapter Six: Superhero Camouflage

Meg lay down on her bedroom floor, a notebook in front of her and the dress-up bin by her side.

She had been doing a lot of thinking about superheroes and how they disguise their identities to protect themselves and those they love. Most of them wore full-body costumes, some with capes, some with masks, and some with both.

Meg opened the notebook, tapping a pencil on the blank page. While costumes may have worked for superheroes in movies, they weren't possible in real life. She imagined changing into a full costume before jumping into the sinkhole to rescue Caroline. The little girl would have fallen to the bottom of the pit before Meg could have disguised herself. Besides, where would she carry a costume like that? And how would she change without anyone seeing her?

Meg wrote some notes on the page. Whatever disguise she used would need to be small enough to carry around with her, smaller even than a backpack. She remembered the fanny pack she had bought with her birthday money last summer.

She stood and walked to her dresser, rummaging  through the second drawer, where she kept her socks, pajamas, and a handful of treasures. There, tucked in the back corner next to a prism Aunt Nikki had given her and a locket from Grandma Buckland, was the blue-and-yellow, reversible fanny pack that clasped around her waist. She tried it on, adjusting the strap so it fit snugly.

SNAP!

This was great! As long as her disguise fit into this pouch, Meg could carry it with her everywhere.

She went back to her spot on the floor and began digging through the dress-up bin to find things that would fit inside the pack.

She made a small pile of items: false crooked teeth, a curly orange wig, sunglasses, an enormous pink bow tie, a red-and-gold head scarf, and a visor with fake brown hair frizzing up at the top. Meg examined the items, placing pieces together to see what she thought of the different combinations.

Smiling at her final selection, she stuffed her new disguise into her fanny pack and buckled it across her body like a sash. Meg stood in front of the mirror behind her closed door. Testing to see how quickly she could put it on, she unzipped the fanny pack, wrapped the red-and-gold head scarf over her hair, and slipped on the sunglasses.

Meg posed for herself, hands on hips, and
turned to see how she looked from the side.
Perfect!

Chapter Seven:
Undercover Superpowers

Meg was supposed to meet Ruby and Tara at the sinkhole park on Saturday so the girls could examine the filled holes. But Meg was so excited to try out her new disguise that she left thirty minutes early to see if there might be a chance for her to use it.

Meg's mom agreed to let her go alone, even though Curtis had begged to go, too. Mom understood the importance of good old-fashioned girl time and warned her to call if they ended up going to Tara's or Ruby's house instead.

Patting her fanny pack as she hit the sidewalk, Meg skipped to the park, happy that her mom and Curtis hadn't questioned her new accessory. So far, so good.

A handful of little kids roamed the playground, their moms watching from nearby benches. Meg walked around them and into the woods, stopping when she reached the small clearings where the sinkholes used to be. Both holes had been filled in, marked on top by mounds of dark earth. Meg tentatively stepped onto one of the circles with her sneaker, testing to make sure it was steady. She stayed aboveground.

As Meg searched the area for new sinkholes, she heard yelling from the other side of the trees. Following this new noise, she came to the end of the woods where it opened into a small, sandy field.

Watching from behind a thick tree, Meg spotted four boys trying to pull their friend out of the ground. Meg rubbed at her eyes, not sure what she was seeing. The boy seemed to have been swallowed by the sand! Everything below his waist was somehow stuck underground. And he was sinking.

It was quicksand, Meg realized. The boy was stuck in quicksand!

Her heart flapped around in her chest like a startled bird. This was her chance!

Meg unzipped her fanny pack and put on her disguise, her fingers trembling a bit as she tied the head scarf. She brushed down her shirt before stepping from the trees and approaching the boys.

"Can I help?" Meg asked. All the boys turned to look at her, even the one stuck in the ground. Some of them were her age, and she even knew a few from her classes at school.

Despite the seriousness of the situation, they studied Meg, their dazed expressions passing from her scarf to her sunglasses to her fanny pack and back again.

"Who are you?" Tom, a lanky kid from her math class, asked. Meg adjusted her scarf a bit and hoped he wouldn't recognize her.

"A friend," Meg answered. And then, to force them from their quiet stupor, she quickly added, "We don't have a lot of time. Let's get to work."

Chapter Eight: Outwitting Quicksand

The boys turned back to their friend, yanking on his arm and trying to jostle him free. Meg watched in horror as their efforts seemed to be making him sink even deeper.

"STOP!" she yelled. They turned to look at her again, and she explained, "It's not helping. He's getting more stuck."

"So what do we do?" Tom asked.

"Let me think," she said, rewinding through all the science lessons Mr. Fester had taught her class about natural phenomenon. He had talked a little about quicksand, explaining that the most natural human response to it was not the most helpful. You had to relax and avoid panic.

"What's your name?" Meg asked the boy.

"Ethan," he whimpered. The quicksand had reached his chest, and the tears in his eyes threatened to spill onto his cheeks.

"Hi, Ethan." Meg squatted down to look him in the eyes as they talked. "Take deep breaths and float on your back, like you do in the water. That way you won't sink."

Ethan nodded and leaned back into the quicksand. His arms gradually peeked above the surface.

"Now," Meg said, "slowly wiggle your legs free. I'll grab a branch to help get you out."

Meg studied the trees. She super-jumped into the air and accidentally sailed high over a pine tree. She wasn't used to having an audience. On her way down, she grabbed one of the thicker branches and tried to pull it free from the trunk. For a second, the whole tree seemed to loosen in the ground. Meg was afraid

she would pop the entire thing from the earth. But then the branch snapped away, and she dropped back down. The ground shook a bit as she landed.

The branch was taller than Meg and would cover the quicksand perfectly. She jogged back to the group, carrying the branch under one arm.

Ethan's friends continued to watch Meg like she was a unicorn or a yeti, but she didn't have time to worry about them.

Ethan's legs rose to the surface, his knees sticking out from the quicksand. It almost looked like he was making a sand angel.

Meg dropped the branch lengthwise next to Ethan so it lay over the patch of quicksand like a small bridge. If he rolled onto the branch, he would be on more stable ground.

"Ethan," Meg said. "Can you roll over the branch to the other side?"

Ethan nodded. He pulled one arm free from the quicksand and threw it over the branch. The movement made his body turn toward Meg's bridge, and the group watched as he straddled the branch and then rolled over it and onto solid ground. His friends surrounded him, cheering. And then, just to be safe, they dragged him even farther from the quicksand.

Chapter Nine:
Caught in a Costume

It took a few minutes, but Ethan finally stood up, his body covered in sandy sludge.

He faced Meg. "Thank you for helping." His friends mumbled their thanks too, still looking dazed by the whole experience.

"We should get out of here," one of them said, and the rest nodded.

Tom pulled Ethan's arm around his shoulder and helped him catch up with the group. Meg watched the boys as they limped away. They had just passed by two familiar figures who stood gaping at the edge of the woods, their mouths hanging open in the shape of capital Os.

It was Tara and Ruby.

"Meg?" Ruby asked.

Oh no, Meg thought. Her friends must have wandered into the woods when Meg didn't show up on time to meet them at the park. *How much did they see?*

She realized they were standing only ten yards away from where she had just broken the branch using her super-strength. Maybe she could convince them that she was someone else.

Clearing her throat, she tried responding in a deep voice. "Who's Meg?"

Tara crossed her arms over her chest and glared at Meg. "Seriously? We've been best friends for two years, and you're going to try to fool me?"

Meg shook her head. These were her best friends, and she couldn't keep this from them anymore. She pulled the glasses off her face and the head scarf from her head. "Hi?"

Ruby and Tara looked at each other and then back at Meg. All at once they rattled off so many questions, talking over one another and making no sense. Meg shook her head in confusion, and they stopped.

Ruby nodded at Tara, and Tara went first. "How did you jump so high into that tree and break that huge branch?"

Meg took a deep breath, held it for a few seconds, and then released it in one big blow. "Remember that ring Aunt Nikki gave me for my birthday?" Her friends nodded. "It gives me superpowers."

Tara scoffed. "What?"

Meg nodded, and the two girls eyed her suspiciously. "Okay. Watch," she said. Meg jumped high into the air, shooting out of sight for a few seconds before barreling back to the ground, landing in a crouch.

Then, concentrating for a second, Meg disappeared, walked closer to her friends, and reappeared right in front of them. This time, their mouths were wide open, their eyes glazed over in shock.

"So those tricks you did for our mini-Olympics, and the time you jumped onto the fence to save Dan. . . ." Tara trailed off as she thought back. "And nearly knocking over that marble column at Ruby's house?"

"Superpowers," Meg confirmed.

Chapter Ten:
No More Secrets

The girls had become so quiet that Meg didn't know what to do. She sat down on a rock and waited for them to respond.

"Why didn't you tell us?" Ruby muttered so quietly that Meg had to use her super-hearing to understand.

Her best friends leaned so close to one another that their shoulders touched. Meg could tell that keeping this secret had hurt their feelings.

Meg stood up. "I'm sorry. I was afraid someone would take away the ring if anyone found out."

"We wouldn't do that," Ruby said matter-of-factly. "We're best friends."

Meg smiled. "I know. You're right," she said. "I should have told you. It was wrong to keep this a secret from my besties."

"Let's all pinkie-promise never to keep all secrets from each other." Tara held her fist toward Ruby and Meg, her pinkie sticking out.

The girls giggled as they linked pinkies.

"And," Meg said, "let's also promise never to tell anyone about my superpowers. I trust you two, but the more people that know, the harder it will be to keep this a secret!"

They each promised never to tell anyone about Meg's superpowers.

"Can we be your partners?" Ruby asked as they made their way back through the woods and toward the park. "Or maybe your superhero managers?"

Meg laughed. "Of course." Then she thought about the quicksand and the sinkholes. She had to tell them one more thing. "Since I got the ring, all these weird things have been happening in Plainview— like the sinkholes and the quicksand. I need to find out if they're somehow connected to my superpowers."

"We'll help!" Tara said, and Ruby nodded. "But just one thing."

The girls reached the park and stopped walking. "What?" Meg asked.

"You probably shouldn't wear that silly disguise anymore," Tara said. "It's a little distracting. You'll get more attention wearing it than you would just being you."

"Yeah," Ruby agreed. "You looked like a fortune-teller. It's kind of ridiculous."

The three girls busted into sidesplitting laughter, Meg hooting louder than the rest of them. For the first time since she turned eight, she felt the sweet relief of being completely honest with Tara and Ruby. And even though the magic ring gave Meg superpowers, Meg realized that the super-est things in her life were her best friends.

Sammy Griffin is a children's book author and super-geek who fangirls over superheroes and comic books in real life. She lives in Idaho Falls, Idaho, with her super-geek family.

Micah Player was born in Alaska and now lives in the mountains of Utah with a schoolteacher named Stephanie. They are the parents of two rad kids, one brash Yorkshire terrier, and several Casio keyboards.

micahplayer.com

Dragon twins Ella and Owen are always at odds. Owen loves to lounge and read, but adventurous Ella is always looking for excitement. Join these hilarious siblings as they encounter crazy wizards, stinky fish monsters, knights in shining armor, a pumpkin king, and more!

Harris thinks there's something strange about the new kid at school, Zeke, and that's because Zeke is the new kid on the planet! As Harris looks for the truth, Zeke realizes that he has a lot to learn about Earth and blending in. Will Zeke be able to make friends, or will Harris discover his secret? Join their adventures that are out of this world.

Isle of MISFITS

Gibbon is a gargoyle who doesn't like to sit still. But a chance meeting brings him to an island filled with other mythical creatures and a special school for misfits like him! Gibbon and his new friends get all the excitement they can handle in this magical series!

Tales of SASHA

Meet Sasha, one very special horse who discovers she can fly! With the help of her best friend, Wyatt, Sasha sets out to find other flying horses like her. Come along on their adventures as they explore new places and make new friends.